I0669792

Anonymous

The Laundry Manual

Washing made easy

Anonymous

The Laundry Manual
Washing made easy

ISBN/EAN: 9783337391836

Printed in Europe, USA, Canada, Australia, Japan

Cover: Foto ©Andreas Hilbeck / pixelio.de

More available books at **www.hansebooks.com**

THE

LAUNDRY MANUAL;

OR,

𝔚𝔞𝔰𝔥𝔦𝔫𝔤 𝔪𝔞𝔡𝔢 𝔈𝔞𝔰𝔶.

BEING

A COMPLETE AND PRACTICAL TREATISE ON THE BEST METHODS
OF WASHING, BLEACHING, STARCHING,
IRONING, AND POLISHING.

TOGETHER WITH

RECEIPTS FOR MAKING SOAP, TAKING OUT STAINS, ETC., ETC.

BY

A PROFESSED LAUNDERER.

NEW YORK:
PUBLISHED BY THE AUTHOR.
1863.

INDEX.

WASHING AND BLEACHING.

	PAGE		PAGE
Bleaching - - -	21	Mottled or Soft Soap - -	9
Bleaching Clothes - -	22	New Cloth, Bleaching - -	23
" Liquor - -	22	Scalding Clothes - -	18
" New Cloth -	23	Soaking " - -	13
Boiling Clothes - -	14	Soap, Cold - - -	12
Borax Washing Powder -	18	" Family, very good and cheap	12
Clothes, Bleaching - -	22	" Making of - - -	9
" Boiling - -	14	" from Kitchen Grease -	12
" Drying - -	20	" Soft or Mottled - -	9
" Scalding - -	18	Theory of Washing - -	7
" Soaking - -	13	Washing Flannels - -	16
Cold Soap - - -	12	" Fluids, effects of -	14
Drying Clothes - -	20	" Powder, Borax -	18
Family Soap, good and cheap	12	" Theory of - -	7
Flannels - - -	16	Woolen Garments, to Wash or	
Making Soap - -	9	Clean - - - -	17

STARCHING, IRONING AND POLISHING, ETC.

	PAGE		PAGE
Clear Starching - -	27	Mangling - -	32
Clothes Folding - -	28	Plaiting and Crimping -	32
" Sprinkling -	28	Polishing - -	33
Cold Starch -	26	" Board - -	34
Crimping and Plaiting -	32	" Iron - -	33
Flour Starch -	26	Polishing, Starch for -	26
Folding Clothes -	28	Process of Starching -	25
Glue Starch -	26	Sprinkling Clothes -	28
Gum " to make -	26	Starch, Clear - -	27
Ironing - -	29	" Cold - -	26
" Laces, Silks, &c. -	30	" Flour - .	26
" Shirts -	29	" Glue - -	26
" Shirt Bosoms -	30	" Making -	25
" " Collars -	29	" Polish - -	26
" Woolen Garments	33	" for Polishing -	25
Italian Iron - -	32	" To make Gum -	26
Making Starch - -	25	Starching - -	26

REMOVING STAINS.

	PAGE
Acid Stains - - -	37
Alkaline Stains - - -	38
Boards, to Remove Oil or Grease from - - - -	35
Blood Stains - - -	39
Carpets, to Remove Oil or Grease from - - - -	35
Grease Spots, to Remove from Woolen Garments - -	35
Ink Stains - - - -	36
Iron " - - -	36
Mildew or Wine Stains - -	39
Oil or Grease, to Remove from Boards - - - -	35

	PAGE
Oil or Grease, Remove from Carpets,	35
Stains from Acid - - -	37
" from Alkaline - -	38
" from Blood - - -	39
" from Ink - - -	36
" from Iron - - -	26
" from Sweat - - -	38
" from Vegetables - -	38
" from Wine - - -	39
Stains, Removing - - -	34
Sweat Stains - - -	38
Substances for Removing Stains -	34
Vegetable Stains - - -	38
Wine " - - -	39

BREAD MAKING.

Adulteration of Bread - -	46
Apple Journey Cake - -	45
Batter Cakes, Graham Flour -	46
Bread, Adulteration of - -	45
" Fine Flour Rolls - -	40
" Fruit - - -	46
" Indian and Rye - -	44
" Pumpkin - - -	45
" Wheat and Indian Batter -	45
" " Meal - -	42
Cake, Apple Journey - -	45
" Graham Flour Batter -	45
" Journey - - -	44

Fine Flour Bread Rolls - -	40
Fruit Bread - - -	46
Graham Flour Batter Cakes -	45
Indian and Rye Bread - -	44
Journey Cake - - -	45
Observations on Bread Making -	40
Pumpkin Bread - - -	45
Rolls, Fine Flour - -	44
" Rye Bread - - -	40
Rye and Indian Bread - -	44
" Bread Rolls - - -	44
Wheat and Indian Batter Bread -	45
" Meal Bread - -	42

PREFACE.

In presenting this little work to the public our object is to place before our readers a few valuable recipes, in a neat and convenient form, so that they may be at hand whenever desired, and to give such instructions in the various processes of getting up linen as we are able to furnish from many years' experience in the laundry business, and thus assist not only the wife, mother, and blooming miss, in their (often) rough and tiresome journey of life, but useful to all who will be benefited by the suggestions of others.

These recipes are known to be valuable, and no preparation will be recommended in this work but such as experience has shown to be of sterling worth, and such as may be used with perfect safety according to directions. It was not the original design to furnish any recipes for cooking, but being fully convinced that good wholesome bread is one of the great wants of the age, we have given a few recipes for its production. The process which we employ for this certainly possesses the merit of simplicity, and we have proved it to be the best in the world for all who appreciate health.

Though nothing has been said respecting the use of washing-machines, the instructions here given for washing will not only render their employment more successful, but it is believed that they will enable the housewife to perform this operation without the aid of machinery of any kind, with a saving, in most cases, of fully one-half in labor and wear of linen. Trusting, therefore, that these few pages may be the means of lightening the duties of the laundry, and thus confer a blessing upon those who have them to perform, we respectfully submit them to the consideration of our readers.

New York, *August 4th*, 1863.

THE LAUNDRY MANUAL.

WASHING AND BLEACHING.

THEORY OF WASHING.—Nature is pure. It abhors all things that are unclean. Thus God provided water for the refreshment and sustenance of all nature. One of the chief elements of man is water, and he requires it not only for his daily drink, but for the ablution or cleanliness of his body, and likewise of the clothing worn in contact with it.

With respect to the process of purifying or cleansing linen, various substances are now employed which assist in the operation, but the primitive mode of washing clothes was, no doubt, with water only, and this method is still practiced in many countries. The Hindoos, for instance, carry their clothes to the Ganges, where they undergo the necessary purification in water alone. But this requires much time and labor, and to facilitate the operation, certain substances, called detersive or cleansing, have been introduced by the progress of science among Christianized and enlightened nations which greatly assist in the process. Among these, the principal one is soap; and it is requisite that we should first explain how this material is so efficient.

It is well known that oil or grease will not mix or unite with water; in other words, it is not soluble in water, and since the discoloration of linen occasioned by being worn is partly of an oily nature, it is evident that it cannot be removed by water alone, unless such a degree of rubbing be employed as will injure the fabric in some degree. But the combination of oil or grease of any kind with an alkaline substance is soluble in water; hence, if soiled linen comes in contact with soap—which always contains this substance—the alkali of the soap will unite with the oily particles of the cloth, which then being soluble in water, are speedily removed by washing.

Thus it is easy to perceive that the labor of cleansing soiled or greasy linen will be much less in water containing alkali, as soda or potash, than with water alone, and the fabric will suffer less injury from wear, not being necessarily subjected to so much rubbing.

Wood ashes was one of the most ancient detersive substances, and in places where soap is unknown or cannot be procured, they are still used for the same purposes as soap. All the ashes of burned vegetables contain more or less of the alkali called potash ; which, as all know, is frequently employed for washing. Alkalies, however, when used alone, although extremely effective, are capable of not only corroding or injuring the clothes submitted to their action, if employed in too great a quantity, but likewise of acting in the same manner on the hands of the person engaged in the process of washing. The difficulty of properly regulating the strength of alkalies, led to the invention of soap, which consists of an alkali already combined with or united to a certain proportion of oil or fat of some kind, which so much diminishes the corrosive power of the alkali as to render its use perfectly safe ; and still the excess of alkali in the soap is sufficient to be capable of attracting to itself a little more oil or grease, such as may be found in soiled linen, which combines with the alkali, and being thus rendered soluble in water can easily be removed by washing in that fluid. Thus, we perceive, that when soap is employed for washing, the oleaginous matter in soiled linen is converted into soap, in consequence of the affinity that alkali has for fat or grease of any kind, and all soap, being soluble in water, we can readily understand why this material is so effective for cleansing purposes. From this explanation it is evident that the cleansing effect is produced by the alkaline substance in the soap, and that the strongest soaps contain the most of this ingredient in their composition, and it will also be easy to comprehend why soaps of different degrees of strength are suitable for different purposes. It may here be remarked, that there are many detersive substances besides soap. Among these, are various clays, fuller's-earth, etc., which have a similar cleansing effect, but produced in a different manner from that caused by the use of soap.

By the use of these substances the oily particles are absorbed from the cloth, thereby rendering them more easily removed mechanically by rubbing in water, but no chemical union is thus formed as in the case when soap is employed. Such substances, however, are seldom employed, except for removing spots of grease from dyed fabrics, where the use of an alkaline substance would be dangerous or likely to affect the color of the stuffs.

MAKING SOAP.—A knowledge of the nature of soap being useful to all, especially those who superintend the business of the wash-house, we shall first explain in a general way the manufacture of it.

The various kinds of soap are made of one or the other of the fixed alkalies, potash, or soda, combined with fat or oil. We explained above, that it is the alkali which gives to soap its detergent quality, and which renders it soluble in water. The tallow or fat merely serves to moderate the sharpness of the alkali, and prevent its injuring the fabric or the hands of those who use it.

There are two principal varieties of soap, hard and soft. The former is made of soda and tallow, or oil, and the latter of potash and similar oily matters. When soda and tallow alone are employed, the soap is white; but to lower the price and enable the manufacturer to sell it cheaper, in making yellow hard soap, a considerable portion of resin, and sometimes "kitchen stuff," is mixed with the tallow, but this is not so good. Palm oil is sometimes used for the same purpose, and to correct the smell of the resin.

Soft or mottled soap differs in its composition from hard, in containing all potash instead of soda. The detergent properties of soft soap are nearly the same as those of hard, but in consequence of the latter being nearly always adulterated with earths and resin, the former is the most economical for washing and scrubbing. When potash is mixed with tallow or oil the resulting soap does not assume a solid form, and its consistence is never greater than that of hog's lard; but it is easily converted into hard soap by the addition of chloride of sodium (common salt) in the manufacture. The muriatic acid of the common salt goes to the potash, forming muriate of potash, which is drawn off in the waste or spent lye; while the soda unites with the fat, and forms hard soap. The process is simply this: When the mixture of alkali and fat has been boiled sufficiently for soft soap, or the grease has combined well with the alkali, a quantity of common salt is added, to cause the

2

water to separate from the soap, and to harden the latter, which floats at the top. The fire is then withdrawn and the mass allowed to cool. The waste lye or watery part found at the bottom is now drawn off or removed with a pump. When this has been effected the soap is remelted, and agitated until it has acquired the consistence proper for ladling into boxes or square molds, in which the soap, after it has set or become solid, is cut into bars with a piece of brass wire.

Manufacturers vary a little in the details of their process, and in the proportion of their materials; but it appears that soap cannot be made of a great variety of proportions in the ingredients, for the proportions are what are termed definite, that is, fixed by natural laws; so that in one hundred pounds of hard soap there are nearly sixty-one pounds of oil, eight and a half of soda, thirty and a half of water. When potash is used instead of soda, the proportions are 58.4 parts of oil, 12.3 of potash, and 29.3 of water; so that, in general, soap contains from 8 to 12 per cent of alkali, 58 of oil, and about 30 per cent of water. Hard soap is frequently reduced in value by keeping it wet; by a fraudulent management, it is made to contain 60 per cent instead of 30 of water. In this case, it is found to lose weight rapidly by exposure to the air, a discovery often too late for the purchaser.

In order to cause tallow or fat of any kind to unite with alkali, to form soap, it is necessary that the latter should be in a caustic state instead of that of a carbonate, and to this end it must be deprived of its carbonic acid. This is effected by the addition of quicklime, which attacks the carbonic acid from the alkali, and thus renders it caustic. The lime does not enter into the combination of the soap, but only serves to rob the alkali of its carbonic acid. The soap itself is a compound of pure alkali with fat or tallow, and a portion of water. Other substances may be mixed with it, and frequently are for the purposes of fraud, but they do not form soap, that is, they do not combine with it, or constitute the properties of soap as a body.

The best process, therefore, for making soft soap is simply this :— First, procure good ashes, and for each barrel of ashes, place one-fourth peck of caustic or water-slacked lime in the bottom of the leach; if air-slacked, the quantity must be larger, according to the time it has been exposed to the air. To prevent the water from carrying it off in particles, it is usual to place straw below the lime.

The ashes are then put in and pressed down as each successive layer is added, until the leach is full.

A stout barrel, slightly inclined, with a hole bored through the bottom, makes a good leach. It should be placed on a piece of broad plank, with a gutter cut around it, to collect the lye; and high enough from the floor to set a tub under. The water poured upon the ashes should be hot, until the lye begins to run; and the time that should elapse after the water is first applied, till it passes through as lye, should not be less than twenty-four hours; if sooner, the ashes has not been pressed down sufficiently, and the lye will be too weak. It will continue to run so long as water is applied, but at the same time growing weaker, as the potash becomes carried off.

If the ashes could be perfectly fresh, no lime would be required in the leach; as, when first burned, ashes are caustic, but gradually lose this quality by absorbing carbonic acid from the air. The lime abstracts this carbonic acid and renders the lye again caustic.

If lye is not strong enough to float an egg it will not make good soap; but we have known it to do this, and still cause a failure, if not sufficiently caustic. The latter defect may generally be ascertained by adding a portion of some strong acid, as aquafortis or oil of vitrol, which will cause a violent effervescence—even strong vinegar will do. When this is the case, it shows that not enough lime has been used; and it may still do to apply it. We have known its use to cause success even after the materials for the soap had been mixed together.

Some test the strength of lye with a feather. If it is not strong enough to eat a feather it will be too weak to make good soap, and should be boiled until it has acquired sufficient strength to corrode or eat the feather. When this has been effected, put in the grease, which, after boiling a short time, will all be taken up by the lye unless too much grease has been added, or the lye is not sufficiently caustic. If any grease floats on the surface a little more lye should be added.

If the lye is strong enough without boiling, some prefer first melting or boiling the grease, then adding a pint of lye, afterwards a quart, and so on, by gradual additions, until the soap is made. A barrel of good ashes will make a barrel of soap; but if the lye is strong enough to combine well with the grease, the soap will be too strong, and liable to corrode or injure the clothes. This is remedied by diluting it with weak lye, which should be heated boiling hot, and then well-stirred into the soap.

Cold Soap.—The following is a very simple method of making soft soap where wood ashes are abundant. Some lye is made and put into a barrel, and five or six pounds of grease added to it : any refuse grease may be used for the purpose, as pot-skimmings, rinds of bacon, scraps of suet, etc. Then the barrel with its contents, well-stirred together, is placed in the yard, exposed to the sun and air. In course of time the lye and grease become incorporated if the proportions of these have been properly adjusted, for upon this depends the thickening of the soap. If the mixture does not thicken, more fat must be added, unless there is any grease swimming on the surface. When this is the case it shows that there is not lye enough, and some more must be added.

· In making lye for soap of wood ashes, care should be taken to use none but those of the hard woods, as oak, hickory, ash, maple, beech, etc. The ashes of the resinous woods, as the pine and fir, are bad for the purpose, and the lye will not unite with the fat.

A Family Soap very Good and Cheap.—Those who have no wood ashes, or do not wish to take the trouble of setting up a leach, can make a much better article of soft soap than can usually be obtained of the soap-boilers, and at less expense, with a very little trouble, as follows : Put fifteen pounds of good bar-soap, and three pounds of sal soda into a boiler with water enough to dissolve them ; boil them together until the soap is dissolved, then turn the mixture into a barrel and fill it up with cold water ; stir it frequently while cooling, and let it stand three or four days before using.

Soap, as well as candles, should never be used when newly made, but for economy it should lay by to harden slowly ; if dried too fast it will crack.

Soap from Kitchen Grease or Scraps.—Dissolve and pour into a barrel any refuse grease of sixteen pounds, into this put twelve pounds of potash ; then add two or three pailfuls of boiling water ; stir it well three or four times a day for three days ; then add another pail of hot water ; and when it is set or the fat is destroyed, fill up the barrel with water. If a strong soap is desired more potash can be used. Sixteen pounds of potash and twenty-five pounds of good fat to a barrel of water, make a very strong and white soap.

SOAKING CLOTHES.—Whatever method of washing is adopted, previously soaking the clothes to be washed is useful, and if washing is required to be done in the best manner, the clothes should be put to soak in lukewarm soap-suds, and this operation should be performed with care, as it contributes much to the facility of washing, if properly done, by loosening the dirt, and thus saving labor as well as the wear of the linen. Sufficient water should be used to cover the linen without crowding it much, and the tub should be covered with a rug or cloth of some kind to keep the water warm as long as possible. The suds should be strong enough to raise a good lather by stirring or agitating the linen after it is put in soak, and when put into the suds the linen should be rubbed or agitated in some way until a good lather is produced upon it; then, after soaking two or three hours, it may be taken out and rinsed in warm water to remove the loosened dirt before it is boiled.

Half an hour will do very well for soaking linen that is not much soiled, but when convenient it is better to let it soak longer. It is a good practice to put it in soak on the afternoon previous to washing-day, and let it soak over night.

Soft water is of itself a good solvent, even of the oily materials that collect upon linen worn in contact with the body, but time is required to effect the solution. Every one is aware of the effect of keeping the hands or feet moist for a few hours—the entire external coating of secretion is dissolved. The same effect is produced by soaking for a few hours linen soiled by the excretory matter of the skin. If a little soap is rubbed on such parts as are the most soiled before putting in soak, and the linen allowed to soak from twelve to twenty-four hours, cold water will answer very well for soaking it in; but soaking linen in lukewarm water, having a little soap dissolved in it, is by far the most effectual method. Care must be taken, however, if the linen be stained, not to have the water much, if any warmer, than blood-heat, or it will set in the stains.

To save soap when the water is at all hard and will not make a lather, a portion of soda may be added to the lukewarm water: the best way of using it is to have a jug at hand, with the soda dissolved in water, and to add so much of it as is necessary to render the water soft—the quantity must be determined by experience; if too much is used it will exhibit its effects upon the hands of the operator. When hard soap is used this should be dissolved in boiling water before it is added, in order to prevent any unnecessary delay in waiting for it to dissolve.

On this subject a correspondent writes to the *Massachusetts Ploughman* as follows: " I send the following for your housekeeper's department; I have tried it for the last four or five years. Whoever will soak clothes from twelve to thirty-six hours before washing them, will find they can do without patent washing fluids, etc., and save nearly all the wear of clothes by rubbing too. The clothes may be boiled without rubbing—any more than to rinse the loosened dirt."

The *American Agriculturist* asserts that " the great secret of the success of nine out of ten of the washing fluids, mixtures, and machines which have been sold over the country for many years past, is not owing so much to the inherent qualities of the articles as to the process of soaking, which they invariable recommend. If people pursuing the old-fashioned system of washing will simply take the precaution to throw all the clothes to be washed into water ten or fifteen hours before beginning operations, they will find half the labor of rubbing saved in most cases."

There is unquestionably great economy in soaking clothes and a great deal of truth in what the paper and correspondent quoted above say about it, but we are of opinion that, if the clothes are much soiled and the water used for boiling them in is properly prepared, there is much more economy in boiling than soaking them. Although the propriety of boiling or scalding linen before it has been thoroughly washed may be questioned by some, one trial, we think, will convince the most incredulous that the linen can not only be washed better by the following method than by the usual process, but the labor of rubbing and the wear of the linen in consequence of it, almost entirely avoided.

BOILING CLOTHES.—The next operation after soaking is boiling the clothes, and the water used for this purpose should be thus prepared: To ten or twelve gallons of water add half a pint of good soft soap and six ounces of sal soda, or, half a pound of sal soda and six ounces of good bar soap, and when the water is nearly or quite boiling hot and the soap and soda are entirely dissolved, put in the clothes; let them boil for twenty or thirty minutes, then, in order to produce a good color and to remove the soap and soda that have been used, which, if left in, would occasion a disagreeable smell, take them out—preserving the suds, as it can be used two or three times—and put them into a tub of clear boiling water; then, after they have scalded for a few minutes, look them over carefully, and if you find any dirt it can be easily washed out *without the use of a washboard.* Then rinse them in clear water, warm or cold, and they will be as white as snow.

Should the clothes to be washed require more or less than ten gallons of water to boil them in, more or less of the soap and soda can be used in proportion, or if the clothes are not much soiled, the water can be increased to twelve or fifteen gallons without using any more of the compound, provided the soap is good.*

Clothes washed by this method require no rubbing before they are boiled; for if the dirt does not come out by boiling, it will come out much more readily after boiling than before. The object of soaking the clothes is to remove the loose dirt, and thus keep it out of the boiling suds. Should the wristbands or bindings of shirts be very dirty, it may be well to rub a little soap on such parts when they are put in soak. This is all the rubbing about the whole washing, unless the clothes are very dirty, or there are any bad stains, which it may also be well to rub with soap before boiling.

By this method the finest linens, cambrics, laces, etc., can be readily and easily cleansed, and the coarsest, greasiest, and dirtiest clothes readily and easily washed; and the assertion can be safely made, that it is the best and easiest mode of washing ever discovered. It certainly saves all the laborious rubbing, and enables one to complete a heavy wash in a few hours, and with very little fatigue. Washing-day is too often a day of wretchedness, ill-temper, and gloom. Everything is upset; the house is all disorder, and damp, and ill-temper rule over slop and confusion. Now, if washing be a necessity, duty should make it pleasant; and the very sight of the

---

* Poor, dark-colored resin soap will not do. Any good white, or the best quality of brown soap, may be used. The less resin there is in soap the better; but the brown or yellow soap is frequently so largely adulterated with it, that it can easily be detected by its unmistakable odor. A good way to examine soap, is to rub a small piece between the thumb and finger; if poor, it will have a disagreeable, dirty, or sticky feeling.

clean white things, fluttering on the lines in the yard, should impart to the task a comfortable homeliness. We have tried many of the plans proposed to lighten the labor of washing-day. One plan promised to enable a housewife to complete a fortnight's wash in a few hours, at a cost of only five cents, and without hard labor; but in our hands it proved a complete failure, and we have found by experience that the use of the above recipe is the best friend to the washer-woman ever invented. By it one person can do the washing for a family of ten or fifteen persons before breakfast, have the clothes out to dry, and the house kept in good order, and the gentlemen of the family, as well as all about the house, free from washing-day annoyances, and all without rubbing or machinery. Who would not wish to have such comforts?

Clothes should be divided into two or more parcels before boiling, as the dirtiest and most greasy ones ought not to be boiled with those of finer fabric containing less dirt. The finer, cleaner clothes can be boiled first, or the water for boiling the clothes in can be divided into as many parts as you have parcels of clothes, and thus boil each parcel in its proper time.

It would be well if house-keepers would always keep their dirty clothes thus separated till washing-day, instead of throwing them helter-skelter into one pile or bag; for the foul air arising from the dirtiest, greasiest clothes, always injures the finer ones, and makes them more difficult to whiten. When put in soak before washing they should be separated.

Soiled or foul linen ought not to remain long unwashed, as the dirt is then more difficult to be removed. Some families wash only once a month, but once a fortnight would be better; in the meantime, as just observed, the various articles as they are soiled, should be put aside till washing-day with method, instead of being thrown together in a heap. What has been used in the kitchen and other offices should be kept separate, being generally greasy, or otherwise very foul; and, as nothing is more unwholesome, or more apt to injure the air of a house than collections of foul towels, or rags of any kind, these should, if possible, be kept in some outhouse.

WASHING FLANNELS.—*Flannels*, except those of part cotton, should not be boiled, as it would shrink them. Woolen flannels, if white and soft, should be washed in clean suds, and rinsed in hot water. Coarse flannels, colored clothes, socks, etc., can be washed in the boiling suds, having been previously soaked or not. If a little soap be added to the boiling suds, and flannels or blankets are soaked in it two or three hours, they will seldom ever require any rubbing. The suds should be as hot as the hand can easily bear when they are put in soak.

Flannels, worsted hose, and other woolen articles require particular treatment. It is the nature of all woolen textures to shrink considerably if put into hot water, and it is therefore a good practice to shrink the flannel before it is made up into any article of dress, by soaking it in hot water, to prevent it becoming too small after washing. All flannel will continue to shrink by washing in a small degree, but the Welsh flannel least. Cold water shrinks woolen less than hot, but it is not always sufficient to remove the dirt; the water should generally be about as hot as can be borne by the hands. Flannels should be washed in soap-suds, of good white bar soap, without rubbing any soap on them, and well rinsed in hot water, for any soap left in them will injure the texture. It is a good practice, after washing flannels, especially the first time washing, to put them into a clean tub, and turn on sufficient boiling water to cover them, and let them lie till cold. If flannels are rinsed in cold water after being washed in hot suds, they will not feel as soft, especially if the water is at all hard, as if rinsed in hot water. Woolen socks, after being washed, should be put into boiling water, and left until it is cold, to prevent them becoming hard and stiff.

To Wash or Clean Woolen Garments.—The soiled parts of woolen garments may be cleaned with a mixture composed of one spoonful of ox-gall, two spoonfuls of hartshorn, and two spoonfuls of alcohol, and then sponged over with a towel wet in cold water. But if they require washing, the following compound should be used in a first water, and the above mixture added to the second water. Cut some soap into shreds and put it into a kittle over the fire, with just sufficient water to dissolve it; when dissolved, take it from the fire, and to four spoonfuls of the soap add a spoonful of ox-gall, a spoonful of hartshorn, and a spoonful of spirits turpentine, then stir them well together and put the compound into sufficient lukewarm water to saturate well the garment; but to insure its being thoroughly diffused through the water, the compound must be put into a flannel cloth and washed through this into the water. After washing the garment in this water, it must be finished in a second

2*

water, into which the above mixture for cleaning has been put, and ironed while damp, on the wrong side, with a fine cloth spreadover it. Woolen dresses should usually be taken apart before washing. The colors of merinos, mouslindelaines, ginghams, chintzes, printed lawns, etc., may be preserved by washing as above. No colored articles should be allowed to remain long in the water. They should be washed quickly, then rinsed and immediately hung up to dry. If a tea-spoonful of vinegar be stirred into each rinsing water, it will help to brighten the colors.

SCALDING CLOTHES.—When it is not convenient to boil clothes, or if economy is desired in the use of fuel, etc., they may be scalded from forty minutes to an hour in suds prepared as above; or if they are frequently stirred, and *not allowed to boil*, the water may be prepared with one-fourth, or a third less of the compound than is used in the boiling suds. In preparing the scalding suds, first having cut the soap into shreds, and somewhat pulverized the soda, dissolve these in boiling water, then put the desired quantity of water into the boiler and add the compound, and when well mixed up with the water, put in the clothes—having previously soaked them —let them scald as directed above, then take them out into a tub with sufficient suds to finish them off in the usual way, rubbing them here and there as you find necessary, and rinsing.

Though clothes washed as above may require more rubbing than when boiled, yet it will be found to be a good method, requiring in most cases but little or no rubbing, and thus greatly saving labor and wear of linen.

BORAX WASHING POWDER.—The washerwomen of Holland and Belgium, so proverbially clean, and who get up their linen so beautifully white, use refined borax as washing powder instead of soda; they use a large handful of borax to about ten gallons of boiling water; they save in soap nearly half.

Borax being a neutral salt, does not in the least degree injure the texture of the linen; its effect is to soften the hardest water, it is a good dentifrice, is used for cleaning the hair, and in hot countries is used in combination with tartaric acid and bi-carbonate of soda as a cooling beverage.

Borax is more particularly useful in washing clothes where scalding is substituted in the place of boiling them; but then it will be proper to use it in combination with soda, and therefore the following method is suggested, which will be found to answer a good purpose, and is well worthy of trial, especially if it is desired to wash clothes without boiling. Soak the clothes over night; in the morning put four or five pails of water in the boiler, and add half-a-pint of good soft soap, or one-fourth pound of good white bar soap, one ounce borax, and one ounce sal soda (the soap, borax and soda should be dissolved before being put into the boiler); then wring out the clothes and put them into the boiler. They should scald from three-fourths of an hour to an hour, and be frequently stirred, but *not allowed to boil.* Then take them out into a tub with a sufficient quantity of suds in which to rub them out in the usual manner. Then rinse them, using blue water when required, as usual, and they are ready for drying. Should you have more than one boilerful of clothes, when more water is added, a little more of the compound should also be added. After the white clothes are finished, the suds will answer for your colored clothes, stockings, etc. For nice flannels a separate suds should be made.

A more convenient method of using this soap is to prepare enough of it at once for several washings, and have it ready for use when needed; and if prepared in the following manner, half a pound of it will be sufficient for ten or twelve gallons of water:

Take three ounces of borax, four ounces of sal soda, one quart soft water, and one pound good white soap; or it may be prepared with good home-made soft soap, one quart, one pint of water, three ounces of borax, three ounces of sal soda. The borax and soda should be somewhat pulverized and dissolved in the water, then the soap cut up in thin pieces and put in and simmered well together. It should be kept hot, but not boiling, for one or two hours, or until well dissolved, and then set aside to cool, when a solid mass will be formed; but to prevent it from separating, it should be stirred a little before it cools.

By the use of this soap most of the rubbing can be dispensed with, and it is not injurious to the texture of the clothes. It has been proved that clothes washed in this way are more durable than with the common soaps and the rubbing required in connection with them, while the usual caustic or eating effect of the soap, is greatly lessened, and the hands will retain a peculiarly soft and silky feeling, even after a large washing. It is adapted to most of fabrics, and is thought to increase their whiteness. Its cheapness recommends it to all housekeepers.

DRYING CLOTHES.—It is not sufficient that linen is well-washed, if it be not likewise dried in the best manner, since the whiteness and good appearance depend much upon this. The best laundresses usually reside in the outskirts of towns, to have the advantage of drying as much as possible in the open air, where the linen is not exposed to the smoke of towns, which is evidently injurious from the dust and soot which fall and attach themselves to it.

The superiority of washing in India is to be ascribed to the great power of the sun's rays acting upon the linen frequently wetted, which, it is well known, have a powerful effect in whitening it.

But the same cause which renders drying in the sun beneficial to white linen, renders this injurious to all dyed and printed articles, as being destructive to color. These should, therefore, be dried in the shade, and never hung in the sun ; it is the sun's rays, and not merely the air, which particularly occasion colors to fade. Colored articles should, therefore, be dried in a shed, or some place may be selected for the purpose that is sheltered from the sun's rays. Printed cottons not unfrequently suffer considerable injury for want of this precaution, either from negligence or ignorance of the principles we have mentioned. Freezing is also very destructive to colors, and, therefore, all colored articles should be dried within doors in cold weather. But the same cause which renders freezing prejudicial to colored articles, renders it beneficial to white linen and cottons.

In hanging up linen to dry, care should be taken to avoid pailings, or any material that may occasion a stain, especially from iron, as this would cause iron-moulds. Some articles require particular modes of hanging them up to dry. Very thick articles, as quilts, waist-coats, etc., should be hung over two lines placed a few feet apart, so that both sides may be sufficiently exposed to the air. Laces and lace veils require to be stretched smooth, and tacked to a piece of white linen before they are hung up. Muslin and other dresses should be stretched as smooth as possible, that they may not get wrinkled in drying. But it is unnecessary to detail all the little precautions to be observed in hanging out various articles of dress, since these are sufficiently understood by those who are practiced in it, and scarcely admit of being explained by any short directions.

BLEACHING.

In consequence of the great advancement of the science of Chemistry, most of the arts depending upon it have undergone great changes, and all have been more or less improved; but there is not one, perhaps, which has received such apparent benefits from scientific research, and the time of the whole operation so much expedited as that of bleaching.

The most ancient mode of performing this process, and, indeed, the only one formerly known, consisted in exposing the cloth on the grass, where it was subjected to the combined action of frequent wetting, of the air, and the rays of the sun. The origin of bleaching is said to belong to Holland, where most of the brown linen manufactured in Scotland for a long period was sent to be bleached, and to the present day retains the name of "Brown Holland," from that fact. After some preparatory processes, the linen was spread out in bleaching grounds, and sprinkled with pure water several times a day. It required several months' exposure to air, light, and moisture, before the goods were bleached. Goods forwarded to Holland from Scotland, in the month of March, were usually returned in the following October; but, if sent at a later period, were not returned until the autumn of the following year.

By the modern discoveries in chemistry, a new bleaching agent has been introduced which is capable of giving astonishing rapidity and perfection to this important art. This new agent, which possesses the singular property of destroying all vegetable colors, is called chlorine. By its use the same materials, which were formerly submitted to a tedious and troublesome process of five or six months, can now be rendered as perfectly white and free from dirt in a less number of days; and in consequence of this, the old method of bleaching is now almost entirely superseded by the improved process.

There are various methods of bleaching, but the cheapest and best process we have ever tried for restoring clothes to their original whiteness, which have become yellow and full of stains from injudicious washing, lying by, or any other cause, is by the use of chloride of lime and sal soda, in the proportion of five ounces of the former to six of the latter, as given in the following recipe for making

BLEACHING LIQUOR.—Take of chloride of lime, five parts; sal soda, six parts; boiling water, half as many gallons as you have ounces of chloride of lime; put the chloride of lime into any con venient vessel, and pour about two-thirds of the water on to it, let it stand for five or ten minutes, stirring it well; then add the soda. After the soda is dissolved, let it stand for a few minutes to settle, then pour off the liquid and add the rest of the water to the settlings; stir it up well, then let it settle and pour off the liquid carefully from the dregs, and strain the solution through a flannel cloth, or two thicknesses of new cotton cloth, being careful to keep out every particle of the settlings. The water might all be added to the chloride of lime at once, but by adding a part at a time, as directed above, it is believed that it will be more effectual in dissolving or extracting the full strength of the chlorine.

This liquor is an excellent fluid for taking out mildew and stains, as well as bleaching, and in consequence of its great utility and cheapness, it will be advisable for every family to have some of it on hand ready for use. By exposure to the air or light, chloride of lime or the bleaching liquid loses its strength or chlorine; but the solution may be kept in well-corked bottles, in a dark place, for any length of time, and it can be used several times, or until it loses its strength by exposure to the air and light. Most of stains in linen can be taken out by soaking the stained part for a few minutes in this liquid, but as some bad stains, as leather stains in cotton socks, etc., will require a stronger liquor, or to be kept some time wetted with this, to remove them entirely, it will be a better way to make the solution or bleaching liquid twice as strong as it is needed for bleaching, and keep some of it for taking out stains; and when used for bleaching it can be diluted at discretion with cold water.

BLEACHING CLOTHES.—After the clothes have been well washed and rinsed they should be soaked from three to twelve hours in the bleaching liquid; then wrung out, scalded, rinsed, and dried. Very fine goods should not be soaked more than one or two hours. If once soaking does not render the clothes white enough, the same process may be repeated, or they can remain longer in the liquor; but it is not advisable to let them soak over twenty-four hours without rinsing and drying, as it might injure them. Soaking articles for ten or twelve hours in this liquor will take out mildew, but if there are any stains which do not come out, the stained parts should be soaked for fifteen or twenty minutes in some liquor twice as strong as this, and then, without rinsing, the articles should be soaked again for a few hours in the bleaching liquid. Should it not be conveniet to scald and rinse the clothes when they are wrung out of the bleaching liquid, they may be put into cold water till it is. If it is cold enough to freeze the clothes when they are hung out to dry, they will be all the whiter for it.

BLEACHING NEW CLOTH.—The bleaching of cotton and linen, in the first instance, being now almost always performed by the manufacturer, does not come within the scope of domestic economy, and therefore need not be treated of here much in detail. When cotton cloth comes from the loom it is covered with light hairy filaments, which are singed off by passing the web over a heated copper cylinder.

The bleaching is now generally performed with chlorine, and after it is completed, to improve its appearance, it is usually passed through starch made of wheaten flour, mixed with porcelain clay and calcined gypsum or whiting, by which the cloth is made stiffer, and to exhibit greater substance apparently, than it proves to have after being washed. The process was originally contrived for the purposes of fraud; and though now too generally understood to deceive many persons, yet the practice ought to be laid aside. The cloth is then dried on cylinders heated by steam, and afterward calendered, folded, and pressed.

Cotton and linen cloth, as it comes from the loom, is charged with the weaver's dressing, which is a paste of flour and water brushed into the yarn, to render the stretching of the warp more easy. This paste must be removed before bleaching. To discharge it, the cloth must be steeped in cold water for forty-eight hours, until the paste is decomposed by fermentation, which does not extend to the cloth itself. Boiling it in water will not answer, since paste is not soluble in boiling water. To separate the matter that discolors the cloth is properly the business of bleaching. The coloring matter of linen and cotton cloth is of a resinous nature, insoluble in water, and, from its intimate union or dissemination through the very fibres of the cotton and flax, is difficult of separation, even by those substances which have a solvent power over it. Alkaline lyes, or solutions of alkali, rendered caustic, have the property of dissolving resins; hence they have been employed as menstrua for this purpose, but alone they are not sufficient.

It is necessary, therefore, to proceed in the following manner: The cloth to be bleached must first be deprived of the weaver's dressing, by soaking in cold water, and after this well washed and rinsed; it must then be laid for twelve hours in a lye formed of one pound of soda to two gallons of boiling hot water; then it must be boiled for half an hour in the same liquor. A liquor must now be made by mixing chloride of lime with water, in the proportion of four gallons of water to a pound of chloride of lime, which must be well shaken in a stone jar for three days, then allowed to settle, and being drawn off clear or strained, the cloth must be steeped in it for twenty-four hours, then washed in the usual way. If once soaking does not render the cloth sufficiently white, these processes may be successively repeated till it has acquired the necessary whiteness; afterwards, to improve its appearance, the cloth may be steeped in some acid liquor and then washed again with soap.

Sulphuric acid, very much diluted, may be used in the souring process, or it may be formed by the fermentation of bran and water, or sour whey may be employed. The cloth may be kept in the souring for five or six days if it is formed of milk or bran; or, only twenty-four hours if sulphuric acid is used. Sulphuric acid is found more convenient, shortening the process considerably and not more injurious. The use of acid liquor is to dissolve any earthy or metallic matter either inherent in the cloth, or accidently communicated to it, or derived from the impurity of the alkaline salts in which it has been boiled.

Though cloth can be rendered a little whiter by the latter process than by the former, it is believed that the bleaching liquid by the first recipe will be preferred in most instances, since it is much more convenient to use, and the cloth can be rendered sufficiently white for all ordinary purposes. When the bleaching liquid by the first recipe is used for bleaching new cloth, it will be necessary to use it stronger than it is used for bleaching clothes, which were made from bleached cloth. It may be used twice as strong, and the cloth steeped in it for twenty-four hours; then it should be well scalded, rinsed, and dried, when the process can be repeated if the cloth has not acquired sufficient whiteness.

STARCHING, IRONING, POLISHING, ETC.

STARCHING.—The process of starching consists merely in dipping certain parts of linen and other articles of wearing apparel into the starch, and after being thoroughly wetted with starch, to pre-vent too much of it sticking to the cloth, and to insure its even dis-semination through the part, the starch is squeezed out, and the part clapped or rubbed between the hands. The parts of linen and other articles of dress that require to be starched are too well known to demand enumeration, and even these vary somewhat with fashion.

MAKING STARCH.—To prepare the starch for use, it must first be mixed with a sufficient quantity of cold water to make it into a thick paste, carefully breaking all the lumps, and rubbing with a spoon till it is quite smooth; hot water should then be added until it is sufficiently thinned to pour easily, then turned into boiling water in the proportion of a pint of water to an ounce of starch, after which it should be boiled for fifteen or twenty minutes, with constant stirring all the while, to prevent burning.

The making of starch properly requires some care. If made in a tin sauce-pan, it will be a chance if it does not burn, like all thick liquids. The best vessels for making it in are a bell-metal skillet, or a copper vessel, tinned, but an earthen-ware pipkin, or a small cast-iron sauce-pan, tinned inside, will answer very well. To give the linen a fine, smooth, glossy appearance, and prevent the iron from sticking, a little white wax, or spermaceti, should be added to the starch while boiling, a piece of either, twice as large as a thim-ble, will be sufficient for a pint of starch. If you have no wax or spermaceti—to be had cheap of any druggist—put in the same quantity of butter, hog's lard, or tallow—mutton is best—or twice as much refined sugar, and boil with the starch. All starch should be strained before using. If it is wanted stiffer than common, a little gum arabic or isinglass dissolved may be added; and for some articles of lawn, gum arabic alone is used without starch. It is also used for silks and fine muslins, but the whitest gum should be selected for starch, as the dark colored might give a yellowish tinge to white goods. When starch is prepared with spermaceti, or if any greasy substance be added to it, the starch should be used before it gets cold, otherwise, perhaps, the articles will be spotted with the oily particles that rise on top of the starch.

To Make Gum Starch.—Take two ounces of gum arabic, pulverize it, then put it into a pitcher and pour a pint of boiling water on it, cover it up and let it stand twelve or fifteen hours, then pour it carefully from the dregs into a clean bottle, cork it, and keep it for use. It can be diluted with water at discretion.

Glue Starch is sometimes used for calicoes. The glue is dissolved by boiling in water, and managed in the same way as gum starch.

Flour Starch.—As an economical kind of starch for articles where no nicety is required, some use common paste made of wheat flour. In making the starch, the flour must be mixed gradually with cold water, so that it may be free from lumps, and thin enough to pour easily, then stir it into a pot of boiling water, and let it boil five or six minutes, stirring it frequently. This starch will answer very well for cotton and linen.

Cold Starch.—To save time, where it is not convenient to boil starch, some use cold or raw starch. This is made by mixing the starch with cold water in the proportion of a pint of water to two large spoonfuls of starch; it is used as soon as mixed, without boiling. Unless constantly agitated, more or less of the starch will fall to the bottom, and hence, if allowed to stand a few seconds, it will require to be well stirred up before the articles are dipped into it. Some prefer cold starch to boiled, but if the ironing is required to be done in the best manner, the boiled starch is the best.

Starch Polish.—Melt equal parts of white wax and spermaceti together, then turn it into a plate to cool.

Starch for Polishing.—Take an ounce, or two large spoonfuls of the best starch, add three spoonfuls of cold water, or just enough to make it, by stirring and rubbing with a wooden spoon, into a thick paste, carefully breaking all the lumps and particles. When rubbed perfectly smooth, add a piece of starch polish about the size of a half-dollar, or equal parts of spermaceti and white wax, a piece of each the size of a large thimble, then pour it into a pint of boiling water, let it boil five or ten minutes, taking care to stir it all the time to prevent burning; it should then be taken off and strained, and well stirred while cooling, and used as soon as cool enough to bear the hands in. The more starch is stirred the better, and if not constantly stirred, both before and after being removed from the fire, it should be covered with a plate to prevent a skin forming.

There are various other substances employed in starch for polishing, besides those given above, as gum arabic, isinglass, whiting, sugar, etc., but, except isinglass, we can see no advantage in using any of them, unless a very strong starch is required, then gum arabic would be useful. Isinglass, white wax or spermaceti may be used either separately or together; and a little practice will show that it does not depend so much upon which of these is employed, or the quantity that is used, as in a proper use of the polishing-iron. If isinglass is used, it must first be dissolved in boiling water, then added to the starch made as directed above. When used alone, about a quarter of an ounce of the whitest and best isinglass will be sufficient for a pint of starch.

It is thought by some that dipping the linen into the hot starch is the best method, while others are of opinion that laying the starch on cold and rubbing it in with the hands is the best way; but we think there is but little choice so long as the cloth is thoroughly saturated with it, except that the most convenient mode is the best.

Our experience is not in favor of boiling starch much for polishing. Some starch may require boiling, but as a general rule we do not boil starch any when made for polishing, more than to thoroughly scald it; and if isinglass alone be used in the starch, it will not require scalding. The isinglass is dissolved in boiling water, then strained and mixed with the starch, previously wet in cold water as usual.

CLEAR STARCHING.—What is called clear starching is the starching of laces, muslins, and other transparent tissues, which requires to be done with peculiar care; for these the starch is made thicker and used hotter than for linens, and the articles, after having been well washed and dried, are dipped into the thick, hot starch, previously strained, in such a way as to have every part thoroughly wet with the starch, and then, to produce clearness, after being squeezed out, they are clapped between the hands. Instead of clapping, which is apt to injure lace, after starching and squeezing out, it should be spread out smoothly on a dry cloth, and rolled up together for half an hour, or until it is dry enough to iron. Muslins and cambrics do not require so thick starch as net or lace. Some prefer cold starch for book-muslin, as some of this kind of muslin has a thick, clammy appearance, if starched in boiled starch. If the articles get too dry for the irons, they may be damped again by rolling them in a damp cloth, but this should, if possible, be avoided. If muslins are sprinkled, they are apt to be spotted; they look well when starched and clapped dry, while the starch is hot, then folded in a damp cloth till they become quite damp before ironing them. All linen, after starching, requires to be made nearly, though not quite, dry before ironing.

It is sometimes found that starched laces and muslins stick to the iron, and to prevent this, it is a good practice to dry the things first, then, after having been starched and dried again, dip them in cold water, and spread them out smooth on a dry cloth, and roll them up together for a few minutes, when they will be ready for the irons; by this process sticking to the iron is prevented. In India, all muslins are starched with rice water, which is said to be excellent, and the rice starch is said not to stick to the irons.

SPRINKLING CLOTHES.—Previous to ironing, all linen and other articles, after being washed and well dried, must be properly folded and slightly damped before the application of the hot iron. The clothes should be sprinkled with clean water, and laid in separate piles—one of flannels, one of colored, one of common, and one of fine articles. The proper degree of dampness is a nicety learned only by practice, but it is essential to the success of good ironing.

FOLDING CLOTHES.—When clothes are folded, they should all be turned right side outward. Starched clothes will usually iron better if damped and folded over night. Shirts will iron well if starched on the afternoon previous to ironing-day, and folded in such a way as not to get too dry before ironing. They should be folded and rolled up, so as to bring the starched parts together inside, having sufficient dry cloth between the wet parts to insure them getting nearly dry before ironing. After being rolled up, they may be sprinkled a little, if necessary, to prevent them getting too dry. It is a good practice, after the small fine articles have been folded, to roll them up in a towel. Sheets and table linen should be shook out and smoothly folded, but not rolled up, since they would require more ironing to smooth the creases out. Colored articles should not remain damp long, as the colors might be injured. They should be laid separate, and ironed first.

IRONING.—Smoothing-irons are employed to give smoothness to such articles of wearing apparel as do not admit of being wound round rollers to be mangled. Mangling is the most expeditious mode of giving a beautiful smooth appearance to linen and cotton, or cloth of any kind, but can only be applied to the large articles, the hot-iron being necessary where there are many folds, or where the texture is too delicate for the mangle.

Ironing is a very important part of what is called the getting up of linen. Bad ironing is known by the creases left, and inaccurate folding, and sometimes by the marks left by ill-cleaned irons. To iron well, it is not only necessary to be dexterous in the use of the iron, but it is also essential that the mode of heating the irons should be effectual.

The proper degree of heat in the smoothing-iron is very necessary to attend to, and no one who is careless in regard to it can ever excel in ironing. It can only be learned by practice, and unless the operator has had considerable practice it will be proper before using the iron, to try its effect upon a piece of cloth kept on the table for that purpose. If the iron is not hot enough it will not properly perform its office, and if too hot, it will scorch the linen. In the latter case, it may be well, not to lose time, to iron some coarse thing that a very hot iron will not injure.

The use of the iron in the various articles of wearing apparal can be learned only by practice under a competent teacher—no verbal directions can be sufficient ; a few hints, however, may be given.

IRONING SHIRTS.—In ironing a shirt, the back or sleeves should be ironed first, then the collar and bosom, and then the front.

IRONING SHIRT COLLARS.—Ironers usually prefer ironing shirt collars that are separate from the shirts to those that are not; but in either case the collar-band should be ironed first, and in order to do this properly, when the collar is on the shirt, lay the shirt on the ironing table and draw the collar-band straight with, and out to the edge of the table, so that the collar being drawn over the edge of the table will drop down out of the way of the iron; by this plan the band can be ironed first and thoroughly dried without the collar being in the way of the iron; the collar can then be laid on the table and ironed as well and easily as if separate from the shirt. Some spread a cloth over such things as require to be very flat in the first ironing, and then go over them again with the iron; but if the starching be well done, and the irons properly heated, this is entirely unnecessary, nor will the things look as well when ironed in this way.

IRONING SHIRT BOSOMS.—In ironing a shirt bosom, care should be taken to have the edges of the bosom straight, so that they will fit well together to button. When the bosom is ironed, the upper side should be ironed first; and to prevent getting one side longer than the other, or making it crooked, stretching or pulling the bosom when it is ironed should be avoided as much as possible. After the bosom is ironed, which should not be done until the collar has been ironed, button or fasten the band together, then if the upper side of the bosom is the longest, pull it down and double it over at the bottom, and press it down with the iron, and if neatly done it will not be noticed. In order to have shirt bosoms set well, they must be properly ironed; and even then, if they are not made well, or are long enough to reach under the waistband of the pantaloons, they will not always set well. In the latter case, if they work up, the waistband of the pants will hold them up, when they will not unfrequently be mussed up, and then they will set badly until they are done up again. This, however, can be prevented if gentlemen will take the trouble, when they put on their shirts, to lay a plait or fold about two inches wide in the bosom at the bottom of it, or where it will come just above the waistband of the pantaloons. The bosom will then, if it works up, work back again without mussing up, and there will be no trouble about its setting well.

IRONING LACES, SILKS, ETC.—Lace and needle-work should always be ironed on the wrong side, and they require a very soft and good ironing blanket to be ironed on; and to be dried by rolling them up, and unrolled as they are ironed. Instead of the common flat iron, some prefer a smooth, round glass bottle filled with hot water to iron fine laces with. When the lace has been starched and dried ready for ironing, it is spread out as smoothly as possible on the ironing cloth, and the glass bottle containing hot water is passed over it, back and forth, as quickly as possible, giving it such pressure as may be required to smooth the lace. Sometimes the lace is passed over the bottle, taking care to keep it smooth. Care must be taken in filling the bottle with hot water, as it will break if the water is turned in too fast. If it is desired to do up lace curtains in the best manner, they should be starched in rice water, into which a little gum arabic, dissolved, has been put, and smoothed by spreading and pinning them out as smoothly as possible on a fine woolen cloth or blanket, which must have been previously fastened to the carpet on the floor, or pinned to a mattress on the bed ; then the doors and windows should be opened to admit the air freely into the room, and the edges of the lace smoothed out with the fingers whilst drying, and when dry it will look as well as new. To iron a white lace veil, lay a piece of thin muslin smoothly over it, and iron it on the wrong side. When silks are ironed, they should be covered over with paper, to prevent the iron from touching the silk, which produces a disagreeable glossiness ; or they may be ironed on the wrong side, when quite damp, with a moderately heated iron. In ironing satin ribbon, lay it within a sheet of clean letter paper (the paper being both under and over it) and press it with a heated iron moved quickly. To iron velvet, turn up the face of the iron, and having previously damped the velvet on the wrong side, draw it over the face of the iron, holding it straight. If the pile is pressed down, cover the smoothing-iron, moderately heated, with a damp cloth ; put on it the wrong side of the velvet; the steam rising from the heated cloth will penetrate through the velvet, and enable the pile to be raised with a soft or whisk brush. In ironing colored articles, care should be taken not to use the iron too hot, as light colors are apt to change or fade, when the iron is used very hot.

Great care must be taken not to scorch anything, for this is in fact reducing a portion of the surface to charcoal ; and though receipts are given for restoring the color, these are nearly, if not quite, useless. If any part of the article to be ironed has become too dry, it must be re-damped ; and should the starch stick to the iron, it must be rubbed on a board upon which a little brick-dust or some ashes have been scattered, wiping the iron afterward. Sometimes rubbing it well on a coarse cloth will be sufficient.

The Italian Iron affords a very neat and expeditious mode of ironing certain articles, as ruffles, that require to be puffed. This iron consists of a hollow tube, and is heated by inserting a cylindrical piece of red hot iron in it, and the things to be ironed are drawn over the iron instead of the iron being passed over them.

PLAITING AND CRIMPING are operations which have long been in use. In plaiting, which is used in ruffles and certain parts of dress, the plaits are first folded with the fingers, in either small or box-plaits, and then pressed down with a heavy iron. Crimping can be performed with much greater regularity and expedition with crimping machines than can be practiced by hand. The process is performed merely by placing the articles between grooved rollers, heated like the Italian iron, and turning them with a handle.

MANGLING is a mode of smoothing linen that gives a more even and beautiful gloss than can be effected by ironing, and the operation can be performed with much greater dispatch; but, except in large laundries, mangles are not much used in this country, partly on account of the room they would occupy, and partly on account of the cost of the machine. In England mangles are much more generally employed than in the United States. Among the furniture of the laundry the mangle is a very important and necessary article; the kind usually employed consists of a large square box, about three feet wide and six feet long, filled with heavy weights, usually stones, which is moved backward and forward upon wooden rollers placed on a strong, level table, with a frame attached to the sides of the table, which serves for legs to the table and to keep the box in its place. The articles to be smoothed are wound round the rollers, which are then put under the box and rolled back and forth till the cloth has acquired sufficient smoothness by the pressure of the box resting upon it. The motion of the box is accomplished in different ways, one of which, and perhaps the most simple, is by means of straps fixed to each end, and passed over a roller which is turned by a crank; the roller being above the box and supported at each end by the frame attached to the sides of the table, and which is made to come above the top of the box. A better way of effecting this is by means of gear, by which the operator always keeps turning the crank the same way. In consequence of this, and a fly-wheel being added to equalize the motion, the labor of working the mangle is greatly diminished.

Another very simple mangle consists of two rollers placed near each other, around one of which the linen is wound, and smoothed by making the other roller press against it while the roller containing the linen is being turned by the crank. The rollers are capable of being placed at a distance from each other suited to the several articles, and covered with several folds of cloth to give elasticity to the pressure, and to prevent injury to the fabrics. This kind of mangle has the advantage of taking up but little room, and is not expensive; but in laundries where expedition is required, the large box-mangle is preferable.

IRONING WOOLEN GARMENTS.—To iron or press any kind of woolen goods, spread several thicknesses of flannel over the press board, on this lay the right side of the fabric, and press it on the wrong side with a damp cotton cloth spread over it. The seams of all woolen garments should be pressed in this way. The knees of pantaloons, or the parts of other garments that have become misshapen, may be restored to their proper shape in the same way.

POLISHING.—The gloss or polish on linen is put on with a polishing iron after it has been ironed in the usual way. It cannot be put on with the face of the iron, therefore the edges of polishing irons are made beveling, and the rounded edge of the iron is used instead of the face.

The shirt bosom or collar to be polished is laid on a hard, smooth surface or polishing board, and rubbed with a fine, damp cloth, or a piece of fine, soft sponge, just sufficient to moisten the surface of the cloth without wetting it through, and then polished by ironing or rubbing back and forth with the edge of the iron moderately heated, giving it such pressure as is required to put on the polish. After a little practice the iron may be used as hot for polishing as for ironing.

Very much depends upon properly damping the surface of the cloth and giving the iron sufficient pressure. The polish is put on by pressure and friction, hence the reason of the edge of the iron being used instead of the face, because the smaller the bearing the greater the pressure. The articles to be polished should be well dried, after ironing, before polishing them.

3

POLISHING IRON.—A four or five pound smoothing-iron with the heel-edge rounded off, makes a good polishing iron. It can easily be ground off on a grind-stone. When used for polishing, this kind of iron should be held heel forward, or the reverse from when used for ironing, and, of course, the rounded edge should be used instead of the face.

POLISHING BOARD.—A piece of pine board eight or nine inches wide and about twenty inches in length, smoothly planed and covered with one thickness of flannel, and over this with one or two thicknesses of cotton cloth drawn smoothly and very tightly, makes a good polishing board. The flannel should not be too coarse, it should be a rather fine, thick, and firm piece.

REMOVING STAINS.

SUBSTANCES FOR REMOVING STAINS.—Receipt-books give an almost endless number of directions, without the reasons, in the form of a vast, undigested mass of remedies. A knowledge of the substances, and the application of chemical principles, greatly simplify the act, and render intelligible and certain what before was only accomplished by guess-work and endless trials.

In removing spots and stains, regard must be had to the nature of the cloth that is stained, and also to that of the matter which produced the spot, since it is desirable to remove the stain, without affecting the original color. To remove any matter from cloth we must find some substance capable of dissolving it without injury to the cloth. Fat, oils, and grease are dissolved by alkalies, soap, ox-gall and essential oil of turpentine; or they may be absorbed by chalk, fuller's-earth, blotting-paper, etc. The choice of these will depend upon the nature of the cloth that is stained. Soap or alkali, for instance, will readily remove grease, but they will also discharge the colors of many dyed stuffs, therefore the absorbent earths, ox-gall, and essential oil of turpentine are employed to remove grease where an alkali would be dangerous. Ox-gall dissolves the grease without injuring the stuffs or affecting the colors generally. Sulphuric ether is a powerful solvent for oils and resins, and does not affect the colors, but is so volatile that it leaves what it has dissolved too soon. The essential oil of turpentine is one of the most convenient agents for removing oil or grease, wax and resin, and it does not affect the stuffs nor the colors; and the disagreeable smell it leaves may be overcome by some other essence more agreeable, or by exposure to the air for a short time. Burning fluid may also be used for the same purpose, and in most cases will answer very well. But the best of all is the new preparation termed *Benzine*, which excels anything else we know of in efficiency.

To Remove Spots of Grease or Paint from Woolen Garments, etc.—Wet the spot with a few drops of benzine, and rub it quickly between the fingers. Oil spots and stains from candle snuffs, on woolen table covers, paint spots on garments, etc., are thus perfectly removed without the slightest discoloration.

Magnesia, moistened, and rubbed on grease spots, and, when dry, brushed off, will sometimes remove them. Fuller's-earth is sometimes employed for the same purpose. This earth, wet with hot water, is laid upon the spot, and as the water evaporates the oil will be absorbed, and the whole may then be removed by brushing.

To Remove Oil or Grease from Carpets.—Take blue clay, such as potters use, spread it pulverized on the spot, spread a newspaper over the clay, then to keep all in place, throw a mat over it, let it remain in this state some two weeks, changing the clay once or twice in the meantime, and the spot will entirely disappear. In place of blue clay, buckwheat meal may be used, which is said to be equally as good. It may also be used for extracting oil or grease from any woolen fabric merely by rolling the meal up in the cloth; but if the stains are not recent, it should be laid by for several days with something upon it to press it tightly.

To Extract Oil or Grease from Boards.—Wet fuller's-earth with hot water, and let it stand till it is cold, then spread a thick plaster of this over the spots, let it remain on ten or twelve hours, then scour the place with hot water. If once is not sufficient, repeat the process; or the fuller's-earth may be mixed with pearlash and water so as to make a paste, and this spread upon the stain: take equal parts of fuller's-earth and pearlash—a quarter of a pound of each—and boil these in a quart of soft water, and, while hot, spread it on the spots, let it remain on all night, next day scour it off with sand or soap and hot water.

Recent Stains of Grease may be removed from boards with flour ; wet the spots with cold water and cover them over with dry flour, which should be changed once a day for a week, when the spots will disappear.

Floor Boarding and other wood work is exceedingly apt to be stained by various substances spilt upon it. Ink stains, for instance, are exceedingly obstinate, they withstand washing many times, and at last turn to a rusty iron color from the application of the alkali of the soap. But the black stain of recent ink and the rusty iron-mold may be removed by the action of oxalic or muriatic acid. As wood is not likely to be injured like cloth or linen, the latter may be used, being the cheaper, and it should be diluted with two or three times its bulk of water, and applied until the stain is removed. Grease which has been trodden in, or has remained a long time, should be first softened by the application of a little turpentine, and then it will be found to yield much more readily than it otherwise would to the action of fuller's-earth and pearlash or soda. Chamber-lye turned on the spots, boiling hot, and afterwards scrubbed with soap and water, will also remove them. Fruit stains are quickly removed by the action of a little chloride of lime, mixed with water, and applied until the desired effect is produced. It should be borne in mind, however, that all vegetable colors are utterly destroyed beyond any restoration by the energetic action of this agent.

IRON STAINS.—These come from iron-rust, ink, etc. To remove them, the iron is first dissolved by a solution of oxalic acid in water. The oxalate of iron thus produced, which, unlike iron-rust, being soluble, is easily washed away. Ink spots, tanno-gallate of iron, upon the printed leaves of books, are removed in the same way, but the lamp-black of the printer's ink is not at all affected. If fresh, such spots may be wholly effaced; if old and dry, a very little will remain.

Wheel grease makes a compound stain of grease and iron. The grease may be taken out first with alkali, then the iron with oxalic acid. If tar has been used on the wheel, rub on lard, which will dissolve it, and then apply the alkali. Turpentine will answer nearly the same purpose as lard.

INK STAINS.—Recent stains of ink may be removed, if before the ink is dry the places be washed with sweet milk; if this does not succeed, rub the part with vinegar, sorrel, or lemon juice, or tartaric acid, and afterward wash it with soap and water. Ink or iron stains may also be removed by the bleaching liquid already described.

The following recipe for the same purpose has been given in Webster's Encyclopedia: "The black color of ink is owing to red oxyd of iron united to a principle existing in all barks, called gallic acid; and iron-molds are the red stains of iron, owing to the red oxyd of iron which is left by itself, from ink, or from contact with rust of iron. Whatever dissolves the iron will destroy the iron mould; acids have this effect, but if they are too strong they likewise corrode the linen. Certain weak acids, which have a strong affinity for iron, are selected for this purpose; the best of which is the citric acid, or the acid found naturally in the citron, in limes, in lemons, and other fruits. On account of its having been procured plentifully from lemons, it is sometimes called *salt of lemons*, or crystallized lemon juice.

"Another acid which has the same effect, and which is now more used, from being cheaper, is the *oxalic acid*, which, it is proper to know, is a deadly poison. This acid exists naturally in wood sorrel; though in this plant it does not exist pure, but combined with potash, forming oxalate of potash, which is also poisonous. The leaves of the wood sorrel, which contain in their grain this oxalate of potash, when bruised and rubbed upon iron-molds, remove them; but as a more convenient mode, this salt has been extracted from sorrel, and is sold for this purpose, under the very improper name of salt of lemons.

"The method of taking out iron-molds with salt of lemons, whether the genuine or the fictitious, is this: A small quantity of the salt is pounded and applied on the spot, and then some hot water is dropped on it, and rubbed in, upon a pewter plate, placed upon a stove, or on a water-plate containing boiling water; the acid dissolves the iron in the iron-mold, or the ink, and a little warm water washes all out. If once is not enough, it must be done over again. The rationale of this effect is, that the oxalic acid has a greater affinity for iron, leaving the potash, and forming an oxalate of iron, which salt is colorless, and being soluble, is easily washed away."

ACID STAINS.—When stains are produced by acids, alkalies, or any liquids containing these, the color of the stuff is acted upon and changed. The color may sometimes be restored by the application

3*

of something that would have a neutralizing effect; for an acid an alkali, and for an alkali an acid; but this cannot be effected unless the acid or alkali was very weak. Acid stains may generally be known by reddening black, brown, and violet dyes, and all blue colors except Prussian blue and indigo. Yellow colors are generally rendered paler, except the color annatto, which becomes orange. These stains, as just observed, are neutralized by alkalies. A spot, for instance, on a woolen coat, from sulphuric acid, or strong vinegar, may be entirely removed by applying a solution of saleratus. Apply it cautiously till the acid is exactly neutralized, which may be known by the restoration of color, and then sponge off the salt thus made by means of a sponge. Ammonia is still better for delicate fabrics.

Sweat Stains are chiefly occasioned by a little muriate of soda and acetic acid, which produce nearly the same effects as acids generally, and are to be removed in the same way, operating cautiously.

Alkaline Stains.—These are the opposite of acid stains; they change vegetable blues to green, red to violet, green to yellow, annatto to red, and yellow to brown. They are to be treated with acids, and the same observations which were made with respect to the use of alkalies in removing acid stains will apply to the use of acids in removing alkaline stains.

Vegetable Stains.—These include fruit stains, and may be removed by merely washing, if that can be done before the stain is dry, but after that the coloring matter adheres with more force, and is sometimes difficult to remove. If the stain be recent, it may be removed sometimes by rubbing on a little alkali, as pearlash or soda; but a mixture of ammonia and alcohol is safer; the spots should be soaked in it some time. Diluted muriatic acid, two parts water to one of the acid, will frequently succeed. Soak the stained part two or three minutes, and rinse in cold water. Some faint stains may be removed by sour buttermilk.

If the fruit stains have been long in, rub the stains on each side with yellow soap, then mix some starch to a thick paste with cold water, and spread it over the soaped places and rub it well in; hang the linen in the air, exposed to the sun, for three or four days, and, if this be not sufficient, rub off the mixture, and repeat the process with fresh soap and starch.

MILDEW OR WINE STAINS.—To take out mildew, wet the article and rub the mildewed part well with soap, then rub powdered chalk thickly on, and lay it in the sun ; when it dries wet it again, and after wetting and drying two or three times the mildew will usually disappear, but sometimes it may be necessary to repeat the process next day with fresh soap and chalk. Wine stains can be removed in the same way. Soaking linen in lime water will remove mildew, but it must not be too strong as it will corrode the linen. If allowed to soak for ten or twelve hours, two ounces of lime to a gallon of water will answer the purpose. It may also be removed by the bleaching liquid. (*See Bleaching.*)

BLOOD STAINS.—These are sometimes difficult to remove by washing; when this is the case they can quickly be dispelled by soap and chamber-lye. Wet the stains in chamber-lye and rub on a little soap and they will soon disappear, when the whole can easily be removed by washing, or the soap and chamber-lye can be mixed together and rubbed on the stains, a few minutes before washing, which will also remove them.

The most effectual thing for removing stains of all kinds, except those from grease, is the bleaching liquid. This solution will remove any stains from linen by keeping the part some time wet with it ; but it has no effect upon grease or oil. But it should be remembered that this liquid will also remove any other vegetable color which may have been used for dyeing the fabric.

To remove stains from calico or other colored substances, without affecting the original hue, requires not only a knowledge of the materials used in dyeing, but of those which will dispel the stain without affecting these dyes, and would be too extended a subject for our present limits.

It will be proper whenever any preparation is used for removing stains from cloth, to try its effect upon a piece of the fabric, to see if it will answer the purpose without injuring the cloth or the color, for the directions for using many of the remedies that are recommended are so vague, that they will not only prove to be useless in the hands of those unaccustomed to them, but will not unfrequently do more harm than good.

BREAD MAKING.

BREAD has been emphatically termed the " staff of life ;" and the quality of it is a matter universally allowed to be deserving of serious consideration ; for good bread is not merely an article of luxury but is essential to our health. Poor bread is one of the principal causes of indigestion and dyspepsia ; hence one of the great wants of the age is good, wholesome, palatable bread which, while it retains all the sweetness of the grain itself, shall be as light as that in common use and free from any health-destroying mixture. Such bread can be made as easily as any other ; indeed we think the assertion can be safely made that it can be produced with less trouble and expense than any other, and hence all who make their own bread can have it if desired. Good bread has been truly regarded as the " perfection of cookery; " but it should be more distinctly borne in mind than it is that mere palatableness in bread does not always constitute goodness. The more palatable bread is, the better, provided it is wholesome ; but bread may be very palatable and still be very bad. The best bread is that which is the most healthful ; but so many compounds are used now-a-days for raising bread that it has not only become a prolific source of disease but it has well nigh become the staff of death, and could we induce even a few of our readers to adopt this better and more healthful method of making bread alluded to above, we shall not regret having occupied a portion of our space for this purpose.

To treat of bread-making as the subject demands would require all the space this little book affords ; we shall, therefore, give a few recipes for beginners, and leave them to study the subject further at their own leisure. Our chief aim here is to induce our readers to adopt good plans rather than repeat descriptions which they may easily obtain from other sources.

FINE FLOUR BREAD ROLLS.—Wet the flour with sufficient pure cold water to form a rather stiff dough ; then roll it out and cut it into strips, which roll into a round form about twice the size of the finger and cut them into pieces three or four inches in length ; bake ten or fifteen minutes in a *hot* or *very quick* oven ; serve fresh.

Especial care must be taken to have the oven *hot* when this bread begins to bake, as the lightness of the bread depends very mucl upon the heat of the oven. The hotter the oven—provided it doe not burn the dough—when the process of baking begins, the lighter will be the bread.

This bread being free from yeast, saleratus, or other deleterious substance, will be found not only light, pure and sweet, but the most palatable and wholesome that can be made from *fine flour ;* but the most healthful and the best bread in the world is that made of good *unbolted* wheat flour.

Much of the food now eaten is too rich and concentrated. It is a well ascertained law of the animal economy, that food to be healthy, must contain a considerable proportion of matter that is generally considered innutritious. Thus, Magendie, the physiologist found that dogs, fed upon superfine flour bread and water, died invariably in about seven weeks, varying only a day or two. But when fed upon coarse bread, or such as contained the whole or a large proportion of the bran, they were found in no respect to suffer.

Professor R. T. Trall, M. D., Principal of the New York Hygeio-Therapeutic College, says : " Bread, which is, or should be the staff of life, has, by the perversions of flouring-mills and the bakers, become a prolific source of disease and death. Much as the health reformers declaim against the abominations of pork, ham, sausages and lard, as articles of human food, I am of opinion that fine flour in its various forms of bread, short-cake, butter-biscuits, dough-nuts, puddings, and pastry, is quite as productive of disease as are the grosser elements of the scavenger swine.

" Nearly all the bread used in civilized society is made of fine or superfine flour, which is always obstructing and constipating, and which is deficient in some of the most important elements of the grain ; and it is still further vitiated by fermentation, or by acids and alkalies which are employed to render the bread light."

Joel Shew, M. D., an eminent author and practitioner of New York, says : " A host of diseases both acute and chronic, are either caused or greatly aggravated by concentration in food. Indigestion, with its immense train of evils, constipation, loss of flesh, corpulency, nervous and general debility, torpor, and sluggishness of the general system, are the principal roots of all disease in the human family, and these are among the difficulties caused by too great richness of food. Children are often injured in this way. Mothers, in their kindness, think nothing too good for their little ones. Sugar, sugar candy, sweetened milk, superfine bread, and rich pastries, are all given for the same reason. There is great and prevailing error upon this subject, and happy are those parents who take it upon themselves to gain wisdom in this most important matter of food."

WHEAT MEAL BREAD.—Pure and wholesome bread, containing the whole substance of the wheat, if properly managed, can be made as light as ordinary loaf-bread with no other raising than atmospheric air.   To effect this, the dough must be mixed to a proper consistence with boiling water—neither too soft nor too stiff.   It should be made about as stiff as it can be stirred with a strong spoon; then made into small cakes or rolls so as to expose the greatest possible surface to the heat of the oven.   When made into rolls they should be made about an inch in thickness and three or four inches in length.   They may be made larger when the cook has learned the importance of having the *oven hot* before baking. Making the dough into rolls is the best form, as it exposes the largest surface to the heat and forms a smoother and more tender crust, but when a large quantity is required the usual method of preparing it, is, to roll out the dough about three-fourths of an inch thick, and cut it into strips an inch and a half wide, which are then cross-cut into diamond-shaped cakes.   The cakes are rubbed over with flour, and baked about twenty minutes in a *hot oven*.

This bread is raised by the expansion of the air in the dough, which thus renders the bread light, but it is very essential that it should begin to bake with a *brisk heat*; the latter part need not be so intense.   The reason is this : The heat when sufficient, instantly forms a nearly impervious crust over the dough, by which the air is retained, and expanded by the heat of the oven; but if the heat be slow at first, so that a crust is not formed, the particles of air will work out without raising the bread.   To insure success let the dough remain until the oven is just the right heat.

Using hot water to wet the meal with, causes it to swell at once, so that when the air is expanded in the dough by the heat of the oven, the space is not filled by the swelling of the meal, which would be the result if wet with cold water ; but to insure the meal being thoroughly scalded and thus properly swelled the water must be boiling hot and quickly stirred into the meal, otherwise the bread will not be so light.   If the meal is mixed with cold water instead of hot, and allowed to stand and swell for several hours before baking, it will be nearly as light as if mixed with hot water and baked at once.

Few are aware of the delicious bread this simple process affords —unlike raised or fermented bread, it may be eaten so soon after cooked as sufficiently cooled by the most confirmed invalid without the slightest injury. When two or three days old if merely put in a hot oven a few minutes it will have the tenderness and flavor of freshly-made bread, or it will be still more tender if dipped in cold water and then heated. If by accident the bread is baked too long, soak it in cold water two or three minutes, then replace it in the oven, and when warmed through it will be soft and light, and suitable for persons with the poorest teeth.

The merits of this bread have been fully tested, and its superiority over the raised or fermented bread has been fully established beyond all controversy by some of our largest and best health institutions, they having used it exclusively for several years, and thus proved its superiority not only over the fine flour bread, but over the so called dyspepsia bread, which the cook-books give so many false directions for making. A small portion of white bread may be desired in some cases by those who have long been accustomed to it; but the brown, after it is used a short time, will be found more palatable, and conducive to a more regular and healthy condition of the system, and few persons once accustomed to the rich and delicious flavor of this pure article, this true "staff of life," will ever desire to return to bread rotted by fermentation, or poisoned by acids and alkalies.

"Few persons," observes Dr. Trall, "know anything about physiological cooking; and so perverted are the appetences of the masses, that to talk to them of physiological food is very much like talking to a brandy-toper of the beauties of 'clear cold water,' or to a tobacco-smoker of the virtues of a pure atmosphere." This, we believe, is true and pity 'tis 'tis true. But should any of our readers so far overcome their prejudices as to give this bread a trial, and do not succeed in making it as light as ordinary loaf-bread, they should carefully read over the directions, and then try again, for if these are properly observed you cannot fail of getting light bread; but those unaccustomed to making unleavened bread should commence with Graham flour, as it is more difficult to make it light from fine flour.

It may be observed that when bread is light enough to readily dissolve or separate in the mouth, without sticking to the teeth or gums when eaten, it may be considered good bread so far as lightness is concerned; but it is difficult to accomplish this with superfine flour, which is a perversion of the flouring-mills, and is not to be recommended for bread.

To obtain the best bread, it is not only necessary that the wheat should be of the best quality, but that the meal be *freshly ground*. Graham flour is not unfrequently kept too long to be good, and the bread made from it will, of course, be poor, and the failure, perhaps, attributed to some other cause, therefore, when practicable, it should be procured from the mill, or ground to order.

RYE AND INDIAN BREAD.—Rye and Indian-meal may be mixed in any proportions, to suit the taste or fancy. The practical rule to observe in making it is, that when the proportion of Indian is the largest, the dough should be made soft ; but when the proportion of rye is the largest, it should be made stiff. Also, the larger the proportion of Indian and the softer the dough, the longer it will require baking, and the hotter the oven should be.

This has long been a favorite bread in New England, and the following recipe is for the genuine article, which the modern use of poor molasses, yeast, etc., has made so scarce.

Take one part rye-meal and two parts of Indian; pour boiling water over the Indian, and stir it till the whole is sufficiently wet to work in the rye without adding any more water; and when about milk-warm, work in the rye-meal. Should the dough be too stiff, add as much warm, *but not hot*, water as may be necessary; bake in a round iron dish from three to five hours. This bread, when new, or a day or two old, may be sliced and toasted; it is very sweet and wholesome.

The crust is apt to fall off: this may be wet in water and put into a stew-pan with some moderately tart apples, peeled and sliced, nicely covering the apples with the crust; then add a little water, and cover the dish with a tightly-fitting cover, set it on the stove till the apples are cooked, and then take the crust off into plates, sweeten the apples to suit the taste, and spread it over the crust. This is an excellent dish, if care has been taken to prevent burning the crust.

RYE BREAD ROLLS.—Rye-meal may be mixed with hot or cold water and made into small cakes or bread rolls in the same manner as the wheat-meal or fine flour bread rolls.

JOURNEY CAKE.—Mix coarse ground Indian-meal with boiling water, and make it into a thin cake or cakes, and bake in a *quick* oven : or it may be made into good-sized balls, and flattened with the hand wet in water, and baked on a griddle. Some prefer this mixed with cold water to the consistence of ordinary batter for griddle cakes, and spread about half an inch thick in a baking dish and baked in a quick oven. The bottom of the dish should be well covered with meal to prevent sticking. Wheat or oat-meal batter bread may be made in the same way.

WHEAT AND INDIAN BATTER BREAD.—Mix fresh-ground wheat and corn-meal together, in the proportion of two or three parts of the former to one of the latter—white corn-meal is best—then stir in sufficient cold water to form a *very stiff* batter, or a rather soft dough ; let it stand for several hours to swell, and, when ready for baking, spread it from a half to three-fourths of an inch deep in a bake-pan and bake fifteen or twenty minutes in a quick oven.

GRAHAM FLOUR BATTER CAKES.—Mix wheat-meal (Graham flour) with sufficient pure cold water to make it into a rather stiff batter, then turn it into small tins and bake in a quick oven.

Note.—The tins should be about two inches square and three-fourths of an inch deep. If larger or smaller, the cakes will not be so light and sweet. These cakes, when fresh, if properly made, are not only sweeter than the bread rolls, but they are equally as light, and possess the relative merit of presenting a nicer appearance when set on the table. It may here be remarked that the surest way of having light and sweet rolls is to place them on the grate in the stove-oven, instead of putting them into pans to bake.

APPLE JOURNEY CAKE.—Take a pint bowlful of sweet apples, peeled and chopped fine, add a pint of corn-meal, and a large table-spoonful of flour ; wet with boiling water. Bake in cakes three-fourths of an inch thick, in a quick oven.

N. B.—A *quick oven* is so hot that one can count moderately only twenty while holding the hand in it ; and a slow oven allows one to count thirty.

PUMPKIN BREAD.—Stew and sift good, ripe pumpkin, having previously taken out the seeds or not, as is preferred ; but if the seeds are taken out, do not scrape the inside of the pumpkin ; the part nearest the seed is the sweetest ; then take equal parts of pumpkin and meal, wheat or Indian, and stir the pumpkin, scalding hot, into the meal, add sufficient boiling water to make it into a soft dough, and put it into floured pans of an inch in depth ; bake in a quick oven, or if Indian meal be used it may be made into loaves and baked in the usual way. This is an excellent and whole-some bread. Apple pumpkin bread may be made by cutting up some sweet or moderately tart apples, with or without peeling, and adding them to bread made as above. If tart apples are used, a few spoonsful of molasses may be added. Many prefer this to pumpkin bread. Some prefer squash bread to pumpkin, it may be made the same as pumpkin. The flavor of pumpkin is improved by stewing for ten or twelve hours, or even longer, over a slow fire.

FRUIT BREAD.—Stewed apples, peaches, pears, pitted-cherries, black currants, or berries, may be mixed with meal, and made into fruit bread. The addition of a little sugar will convert the article into fruit cake.

Note.—To those who desire recipes for cooking *physiologically*, we would recommend the Hydropathic Cook-Book, published by Fowler and Wells. We have found Physiological Cook-Books to be quite scarce, and with cooks in general the question seems to be not how to make changes in the culinary art favorable to health, or even economy, but rather how far they can render these changes agreeable to our fallen standard of taste.

It should be the aim of every housekeeper to favor, as much as possible, a pure diet and simplicity in cooking. Let every house-keeper originate her own recipes on this basis, and better health will be the result; all that is needed for the purpose is an abundance of plain, good sense, and a love for the profession.

ADULTERATION OF BREAD.

The changes which have occurred in the habits of society have, in a great measure, taken the manufacture of bread out of the hands of individuals and placed it in those of the public bakers, on whose skill and integrity we are now depending for an article which has been proverbially called the "*staff of life.*" This is, perhaps, to a certain extent, unavoidable, in the present condition of things, particularly in large cities, and it being a convenience of no small importance to many persons who are thus freed from what would otherwise be a continual source of trouble, it is well nigh overlooked and forgotten that there are any advantages in private or domestic baking to counterbalance the inconvenience of it. In order to form an accurate judgment in deciding this question, or to determine how far domestic baking is worth attending to, it will be necessary to inquire carefully into the nature of this kind of food, and into all the circumstances connected with its production; but our limited space will not admit of our going farther into this subject than to briefly notice the objection to public baking which arises from the liability of being supplied with an inferior or adulterated article in place of the genuine.

That both flour and bread are frequently more or less adulterated, and sometimes with deleterious substances, there is no doubt; indeed it is said that some white substances have been employed—more particularly in European markets—for the purpose of whitening flour and bread by direct mixture, as chalk, whiting, ground stones, plaster of Paris, bones calcined and ground, which are all very prejudicial. It is very unlikely that these are now often employed as adulterating ingredients, however they may have been, since the means of detecting deleterious substances introduced instead of flour are so simple and well understood, it is believed, that few will venture to use them.

Flour of bad or indifferent quality, or damaged, being sold at an inferior price, is perhaps at present what we have most to dread from dishonest bakers, many of whom use wheaten flour of a quality utterly unfit for human food. As in most other cases, the effects of dishonest trading in bread are chiefly felt by the poor, who too often gladly avail themselves of a cheaper article, which not only proves dear in the end as to its amount of nutriment, but which is often doctored up to improve its weight, flavor, and appearance, with most pernicious compounds. Wheat varies in quality more than most other grains, but the worst, whether naturally poor, or damaged by transport and long keeping, finds a ready market at low prices, and speedily passes into bread.

It is chiefly to conceal the defects of the flour that bakers use alum, and sometimes sub-carbonate of ammonia.

The ordinary adulteration of bread is alum; and that alum is employed by many bakers for the purpose of adulterating bread is certain, since many convictions have taken place of bakers who were found to have it in their possession for this purpose. The *Lancet* Commission in its report on the examination of bread, says: Of eight-and-twenty samples, purchased from various houses in the metropolis, the whole were more or less adulterated with alum. Mr. Mitchel avers having discovered as much as 116 grains of alum in a four-pound loaf, while the lowest he found was 34½ grains. This lowest amount is said to be quite sufficient to produce decided effects on the constitution when taken regularly for years together; yet the bakers, when compelled to acknowledge that they use it, excuse themselves by the assertion that it is harmless, and cannot effect the health of the consumer. It is very necessary that we should be extremely cautious how we admit of excuses for the adulteration of so important an article of food as bread, and it is highly desirable that we view the subject in its true light.

Bread that is made from the whole of the wheat is, of course, much less white than what is made of fine flour, but it is more nutritious, and hence the general preference that is given to bread very white has been very properly considered to arise from prejudice, and it is said that bakers have been compelled, in some degree,

to seek out methods of making their bread as white as possible, beyond what their profit will allow in consequence of this false taste
in the public. It is well known that it is impossible to make the
whitest kind of bread light and porous, and of the color and appearance to which the public are now accustomed, of flour alone,
and unadulterated, except it be of the very best quality; and since
good wheat affords a flour whiter than damaged, or than the flour
of other grains, which are sometimes employed for adulterating
wheat flour, as white corn, rice, barley, oats, peas, and beans, it is
no wonder that the public should have the impression that the
whiteness of flour, and, of course, of the bread made from it, is more
likely to be of the first quality rather than what is of a darker color,
since the latter may not only consist of inferior flour, but may be
adulterated with some other substance; but by the use of alum,
bakers are enabled to deceive the public, and to make bread composed of bad flour pass for that which can only be made from pure
ingredients. When the flour is damaged by any cause that injures
its gluten, it is difficult to make the bread rise sufficiently without
the addition of something. The way in which alum acts in covering this defect, as well as that of color, or what may be termed
bleaching the flour, is not well understood; but the fact appears to
be, that a small quantity of alum is sufficient to produce a remark-
able effect. Dr. Ure states that he found the proportions of alum to
be variable, but that its quantity appeared to be in proportion to
the badness of the flour. Dr. Hassell gives the result of a simple
but conclusive experiment as to the use of alum and rice flour,
which shows that the addition of alum enables the flour to take up
more water; the addition of rice enables it to take up still more;
while in getting stale, bread containing alum or rice, or both, does
not part with water so readily as wheaten bread. Thus, we perceive that there are several objects for putting alum into bread: one
of which is to enable the baker to make out of imperfect or damaged
flour a bread that shall look as if it were made from the best flour;
another motive is, that the bread may absorb more water, and thus
weigh more than it should from a certain quantity of flour; both of
which are positively fraudulent. The current proverb as to cheap
bread, "that we may eat of it till we grow hungry," is thus borne
out by an examination of the bread itself.

www.ingramcontent.com/pod-product-compliance
Lightning Source LLC
Chambersburg PA
CBHW021237260626
47172CB00002B/813